The Boy Who Loved
Mammoths

Also By Rafe Martin

Books:
The Rough-Face Girl
The Boy Who Lived With The Seals
Will's Mammoth
Foolish Rabbit's Big Mistake
One Hand Clapping
Dear As Salt
The Storytellers Story
The Hungry Tigress

Tapes:
Animal Dreaming
Ghostly Tales Of Japan
Rafe Martin Tells His Children's Books

All titles available from Yellow Moon Press
Call 1 - 800 - 497 - 4385 to order or reguest a catalog

To Mrs. Berwalt

THE BOY WHO LOVED MAMMOTHS

*Best wishes · Rafe Martin
4.98*

Rafe Martin

Illustrations by
Richard Wehrman

◯ Yellow Moon Press ◯
Cambridge, Massachusetts

ISBN: 0-938756-42-7
Text Copyright © 1995 Rafe Martin
Illustrations Copyright 1995 © Richard Wehrman

Back Cover Photo: Gretchen Howard

Yellow Moon Press
P.O. Box 1316
Cambridge, MA 02238
(617) 776 - 2230
Fax: (617) 776 - 8246

FOREWORD

Though many people know *Will's Mammoth,* my
picture book for young readers, not many know
how that story actually began. Those who have
heard me tell the original story have been
amazed to discover that it's actually a complex
tale suitable for older children and even adults,
not just a story for young children. And they
ask, why did I change it to make it a picture
book? And would I someday do a story book -
one with fewer illustrations and lots of words -
the way I originally wrote it, the version my
telling is actually based upon? Over the years,
these requests have piled up on my desk. So
here, at last, is the story as I originally wrote it
with some terrific illustrations by my good
friend Richard Wehrman. Enjoy!

Rafe Martin
Rochester, NY - Fall 1995

Will loved mammoths. Their curling tusks, glistening eyes, reddish-brown fur and round shaggy ears all seemed magical to him. At night, herds of mammoths strode through his dreams. They forged through drifts of snow and, with great sweeps of their tusks, exposed the yellowed grasses buried below. Crows cawed, flapped, and hopped all around, pecking at the newly-exposed earth. Will saw lone mammoths, too, trumpeting on hillsides beneath a thousand glittering stars. The silver curve of a river shone below. Cave bears prowled. Woolly rhinoceros wandered. Sabre tooth tigers fled. Solid

as boulders, humped like buffalo
– but, oh, so much bigger! What crea-
ture other than a mammoth could face
dangers so calmly? "Saber-tooth tigers," Will thought, "just look out!"

In dreams, he saw it all so clearly.
But when he awoke, it was always to a
world without mammoths. "I'm going
to see a real live mammoth someday,"
Will insisted. "I know it. I really will."

That was his wish – to see a real live
mammoth. But his mother and father
would always say, "It's impossible,
Willie. All the mammoths are extinct.
They died ten thousand years ago.
Why not wish for something else,
something that could come true? Why
not wish for a new sled, or a micro-
scope, or a bowling ball. You'll just

make yourself unhappy wishing for something you can never have. Be practical, Will."

But Will wouldn't listen. He just kept wishing for his mammoth.

On snowy days, Will often climbed the hill behind his house. Wrapped in his layers of thick winter clothing, he felt like a mammoth. Standing on the hill, listening to the silence and the wind, he'd hear a truck shifting gears on the highway far below. For Will, the sound became the far-off trumpeting of a mammoth. After a time, his nose and fingers and toes would turn red and cold. Then they would cry to him like little animals. They bit and cried to him like the wind cried, saying, "Go home, Will. It's too cold."

Still he would wait. Only as darkness fell would he retreat back down the hill, the trail of his own mammoth tracks slowly filling with snow behind him. Sometimes he thought he saw mammoth hairs, long and red, on the snow. But when, breathless, he ran to where he thought he'd seen them, they were always just twigs.

Back in the house, the ice on his boots melted in puddles in the hallway. His wet scarf and mittens and his hat hanging by the door all smelled of cold wet wool. In his mind, he added the aroma of the bales of hay stacked in the neighbor's barn, a whiff of pine resin from the nearby woods, a touch of the coolness rising from the stream where it flowed, unfrozen, through the jewel-edged snow. To Will, it was the smell of mammoth.

One winter's day, three crows flew over Will's house. "Caw!" they called, "Caw! Caw!". Flapping their wings, they flew off in a ragged line towards the hilltop to the east. Will watched them growing smaller and smaller. At last, they were just three black specks fading into the clouds and the lightly falling snow. Then they were gone.

Suddenly Will *knew* where he would find his mammoth – and that it would be today.

He put on his coat, hat, boots, mittens and scarf and set off up the hill. The crows had shown him the way. The mammoth would be waiting in the old abandoned stone quarry on the hill's other side. Often, in warm weather, he had climbed down into that quarry. Sometimes he had found

rocks there with the impressions of seashells in them – fossils from long ago. "Yes," Will thought, "that's where I'll find my mammoth."

Crunch, crunch, crunch. The snow squeaked, packing beneath his boots with every step. His breath made a cloud before him. Snow drifted down. Grey clouds closed in, and the sun became a faint, fuzzily glowing circle. Each snowflake fell silently, drifting down slowly. Then the wind began to blow, and whirling snow hid the house which was now far below.

Soft snow wings brushed Will's face. His scarf was shaggy with snow. He could taste it: sour, wet and cold. He was sweating inside his heavy clothing when he reached the hilltop, but his fingers and toes, cheeks and nose,

were cold. He exhaled loudly and shook his head, flapping his scarf like woolly ears.

He was a mammoth: the huge and powerful lord of a white and silent world. On he went through the pine wood, past needled branches mounded with snow, and then down the hill's other side towards the abandoned quarry.

The sky turned iron grey. The snow fell heavily. The sun's light faltered and sat like a raven among the trees. A cold wind blew, making the falling snow whirl upwards even as it fell. Will came to the edge of the quarry and looked down into the pit. Among the snow-covered heaps of gravel and crumbling stone lay the rusting hulk of an old truck. Piles of reddish, rusted,

flaking iron cable lay nearby, almost
buried by the snow. The whole quarry
was lined with a smooth white blanket
of snow. Will stood and looked. He
saw nothing but stone, rusted metal,
and snow.

Still, he was so sure this was *the day*.
He wouldn't leave. He just stood there
looking and looking. Wasn't that the
shadow of a mammoth beside the

truck? Wasn't that the trumpeting of a
mammoth he heard on the wind?
"Maybe," Will thought, "just maybe!"

Will walked along the quarry's edge,
peering down into the gathering gloom.
There was nothing more to see. And it
was time to go. It would be evening
soon, and a storm was clearly coming.
The wind was rising. Dark clouds were
moving in.

Will turned to leave, when suddenly, a gust of wind blew. He lost his balance, slipped, and grabbed at the ice-slick bushes with his mittened hands. But it was no use. With a cry, He fell down, down, into the quarry. He hit his head. A wild trumpeting split the sky, and everything went black. Then he knew no more.

When Will awoke, he was lying in deep snow at the bottom of the quarry. His head and legs hurt, and he was cold. The sky overhead was black. Great thick flakes of snow were tumbling from the darkness. Up above, at the quarry's rim, the wind howled like a pack of wolves. Will tried to stand, but his legs hurt too much. He must have injured them, maybe even broken

them, when he had fallen. He had to
get home. He'd freeze to death just
lying there.

On the other side of the quarry was a
road. It had been cut for the trucks
that used to carry out the blocks of
quarried stone. If he could crawl to the
road, then he could crawl up out of the
quarry, down the hill, and home. It
would be a long, hard way. "What
other choice do I have?" Will thought
anxiously. "None. So I have to do it!"

He began to crawl. The snow was
cold and wet. Even through his thick
clothes, cold stones cut into him. The
ground itself was rutted and frozen.
By the time he was across the quarry,
he was exhausted, bruised and chilled.
His legs really hurt.

Looking up at where the road cut through the quarry wall, Will saw that he was in big trouble. The Road was blocked. Whole trees, fallen from the quarry's rim during earlier storms, were frozen into ten-foot high drifts of snow. Ice-coated branches, tangled and sharp as antlers, glittered menacingly. There was no way that a boy with injured legs could get through. The thought he had managed to keep at bay closed in on him: "He was trapped!"

"Mom! Dad! he called, "Help! Some-one *please* help!" But the mounds of snow-covered stone muffled his cries and the howling of the wind blocked them. Feeling completely hopeless and alone, Will sank down into a haunted and feverish sleep.

He had a dream. He was lying alone in darkness, cold, and falling snow. Something big was approaching. He heard the snow crunch. He felt the earth shake. He heard breathing – like an engine chugging and puffing - coming his way. But somehow, he wasn't afraid. He just wanted to see what it was.

Will peered into clouds of whirling snow. A dark shape began to loom. There was a glint ... A flash! Then, a great dark shaggy head – oh! it looked exactly like he had always imagined it would! – peered through the curtain of snow.

It was a mammoth! His mammoth!
Two dark eyes and two huge ivory
tusks shone in the darkness. Reddish-
brown fur ruffled in the wind. Little
round shaggy ears flapped, and a furry
trunk swayed. The mammoth's breath
rose in steaming clouds as it walked
steadily on: closer and closer. It stopped just before Will and looked down at
him. It reached forward with its trunk,
breathed its warm breath upon his
face, and touched him on the shoulder.

Will awoke. He opened his eyes ....
and standing there, looking down at
him, really was the mammoth – just
the way he had seen it in his dream!

The mammoth came even closer,
closer and closer, until it was right over
Will. Its legs, thick as shaggy trees,
blocked the wind. Its long fur hung

down around him, making a kind of cave. Will pulled off his mittens, reached back, and touched the mammoth's leg. It was solid and real. "This *isn't* a dream," Will thought. The reddish-brown outer hairs were cold and wet, but the fur beneath was warm and almost dry. Will warmed his cold red hands in the fur. Putting his mittens back on, he huddled safely against the mammoth's sheltering leg.

There was a cold, spruce and snow, wintery-wet-wool smell; a warm, spicy, burnt-leaf and barnyard-circus-tent smell. The air over Will curled and steamed with warmth even as the snow whirled all around. All through the storm the mammoth stood over Will, protecting him, its hair raised in great bristling ridges in the wind.

The wind died down. Now the snow
fell steadily, silently blanketing the
earth, the quarry, and the mammoth.
In time, the snow stopped falling. The
clouds parted, and there were the moon
and stars as bright as ever. In the deep
blue luminous night, Orion the Hunter
reached his arms towards the glowing
milk-bright moon now almost at the
full. High above the trees were other

constellations. Will recognized Cepheus, The King; Cassiopeia, the Queen; the Lyre; and the Bears. Stars glittered and planets shone.

Such a clear and luminous night! The Milky Way burned and shimmered overhead. The freshly fallen snow sparkled. It seemed as if pearls and diamonds had been scattered all around.

The mammoth shook itself, and the piled up snow slid from its back. It rumbled from deep inside and breathed out a great *whoosh* of breath, making the snow whirl up in sparkling clouds. The mammoth turned its huge tusked head back towards Will and wrapped its trunk around him. It set Will up on its humped shoulders. The it began to move straight towards the glittering drifts and frozen trees.

Will could see moonlight gleaming on the mammoth's tusks, on the drifts, and on the ice-coated trees ahead. The mammoth lowered its head and *pushed*. Will felt its great heart beating. He felt the muscles tightening and flexing, the ribs rising and falling be-

neath him. Frozen branches shattered, splintering like glass. The mammoth pushed again. The ice-coated trees slid and rolled aside. The drifts split, parted, and collapsed. They were through!

Up the road they went, the snow-covered ledges of the quarry sinking steadily down around them. The stars were flung overhead like a net of jewels. The moon sailed high, smiling down from the starry night. Snow shifted and slid from the trees. Except for the *crunch* of the mammoth's feet, the *whoosh* of its breath, the *snap* of branches as it moved, the night was still and calm. Will held on tightly to the great fur-helmeted head and padded shoulders. Already, they were among the high pines of the hilltop.

Will hardly noticed. He was only a boy, but he felt rich as a king. His wish had come true!

At the hill's crest, they stopped. The pines, jacketed in ice, stood silent as sentinels, the branches slowly rising and falling in the wind that was now moving up the hill out of the east. The hill's snow-capped crest, was brightly lit by the moon's light. But, beneath the mammoth, beneath the pines, the shadows were dark. Down the hill, far below, Will could see the lights shining out through the windows of his own house. In the bright moonlight he could even see a plume of smoke curling from the chimney. The glistening fields, roads, and distant houses seemed tiny, distinct. Will gripped the mammoth's fur. He could feel the great

heart pounding steadily, the arched ribs calmly rising and falling. Clouds of breath rose. "Thanks," Will whispered, "Thanks."

For a long time, they stood like that on the hilltop.

Now the wind was rising again. The pines began whispering, the ice-thickened branches clicking together, chiming and tinkling. Brightly-edged clouds slid across the moon. The stars grew faint and disappeared. The calm blue night faded, turned grey, then black.

The mammoth raised its trunk and wrapped it around Will. Then it set him down once more upon the snowy ground. Great flakes of snow tumbled out of the blackness, whirling like feathers.

The mammoth's dark eyes looked
down kindly at Will. Its body was like
a mountain fading into the darkness.
Will could clearly see the fur-covered
trunk, the ivory tusks, the fur-capped
head, the little shaggy ears and the two
great shaggy front legs. But beyond
that it was all indistinct.

The night was *so* dark. Suddenly
Will felt very cold. Then he heard a
voice speaking to him - deep and gentle
and patient - a voice as old and strong
as the earth and hills. The voice said,
"Don't be afraid, Will. You'll be all
right. I must go now. Perhaps we'll
meet again."

The mammoth raised its trunk in
salute. Then, it turned and walked
into the shadows, heading back to the
hilltop along the way they had come,
back towards the quarry.

"Stop!" Will called. "Don't go! If you go now, who will ever believe me?"

"They'll believe, Will," came the voice, "you'll see."

Then the mammoth was gone. Once again, Will was alone with darkness, cold and falling snow.

In a minute, he heard a far-off voice calling, "Will! Will! Where are you?" It was his father's voice.

Half-way down the hill, a pale flash-light beam reflected off the whirling snow. The beam, surrounded by the drifting, spinning flakes of snow seemed to be beneath the sea. It was like a diver's light surrounded by swirling plankton specks.

"Dad!" he called. "I'm here! Up on the hill!"

The light turned, came bobbing up the hill, and pointed towards him, getting bigger and brighter. He heard footsteps coming closer and louder, crunching through the snow.

"Will?!"

"Over here!"

In a few minutes, his father was kneeling by his side, concern in his eyes and in the lines of his face. "What happened, Willie? Mom and I have been so worried. I've been looking everywhere for you."

"I fell into the quarry, Dad. I hit my head. I hurt my legs. I couldn't stand up. I couldn't get out. But Dad, Dad –

a mammoth came. He saved me, Dad.
He looked just the way I always imag-
ined he would. He brought me here.
He left just a minute ago."

Will's father looked, but didn't see a
thing - - except snow falling everywhere. "You've got a cut and a bruise
up on your temple, Will. I guess you
hit your head and had some kind of a
dream, son. But you're safe now.
That's all that matters. I'm taking you
home." Then, very carefully, he lifted
Will up and carried him down the hill
to home.

A few hours later, Will was lying in his own bed between clean sheets, safe and warm. Outside, the wind blew. Snowflakes tapped, scratching at his window. One of his legs was in a cast. It was broken. The other was tightly wrapped in an elastic bandage. "It's the kind athletes wear," he thought. Will had twisted his ankle and sprained his knee. A bit of gauze bandage was taped over a cut on his head. Otherwise, he was fine.

Down the hall, Will could hear his mother and father talking in the kitchen. They were washing the dishes and talking about how lucky they had all been. They were saying that even the doctor hadn't been able to explain how Will had ever survived for so long with no signs of exposure to the cold.

Will heard what they said and, at
once, it was all luminously clear to him.
He knew how he had survived. It had-
n't been a dream. It had been true.
The mammoth had really come and
saved him. And he wished that somehow he could make them believe it, too.

Will's hand was clenched tightly. He
opened it. There was a bunch of long,
dark, reddish-brown fur. "Mom, Dad,"
he called, "Look! Come see!"

Outside in the darkness, the earth
slumbered beneath its blanket of snow,
dreaming dreams of the snowy splen-
dors of long ago. From somewhere far-
off came the lonely whistle of a distant
train ... or was it a faint trumpeting, rising even now from beyond the hill to
shatter a silence of ten thousand
years... Listen!

AFTERWORD

There are three distinct versions of *The Boy Who Loved Mammoths:* the original written version, the later told versions, and the picture book that grew out of them. In this book, I present the original version of *The Boy Who Loved Mammoths* as I wrote it more than ten years ago. *Will's Mammoth,* the picture book version illustrated by Caldecott-winner Stephen Gammell, is almost wordless. In my work on the picture book, I saw images in a key - to use a musical analogy - most appropriate for young readers. I had decided that we could be inside Will's imagination, seeing what he sees. When I began working on *Will's Mammoth,* I wrote everything out for Stephen Gammell that I was seeing in the silent places of the story, and then let him *show* us, in his wonderful images, what Will imagines. Part of the beauty of pic-ture books is that they're very much like storytelling. Listening to a story told, we don't see words in our minds, but pictures.

Re-creating a single story in versions for different audiences and occasions is very much a part of the oral tradition. For me, creating three versions of one story is like driving to the same destination by three different routes; I arrive at the same place in the end, but the sights along the way are different. At the end of the picture book, Will is asleep, yet he holds in his hand the flower given him by the mammoth in his daydream. In the written version of the story, Will discovers not a flower but the actual hairs of a mammoth in his hand. In the told version, I have Will's father take those hairs to a museum where he — and we — discover that they are indeed real. The ending of all three versions is pretty much the same: all are ways of saying that the child's dream, the child's imagination, has been REAL.

In all its versions, *The Boy Who Loved Mammoths* grew out of wishes and dreams which began when I was eight years old, growing up in New York City. Back then, my favorite place

was a boulder in my neighborhood. When I
climbed up on it—only good climbers could do
it—it came alive. It was a big gray boulder, and
in my mind it was an elephant. In fact, my
friends and I called it Elephant Rock. It was
shaped like an elephant, too, with a great bulge
for the head, and shoulders, and a slope for the
hind legs and tail. In my mind I can still feel
its smooth worn stone. In dreams, my finger-
tips can still find those hard-won notches,
ledges and grooves in the stone - fingers *there*,
knees press *there*, shift the other hand, hang
by a fingertip *so* - which gave me the gripping
points to work my way up. I can still remember, too, the *thump* as I slid back down the
"tail" and hit the ground.

That boulder had been pushed to where New
York City was later to grow up around it by the
glaciers during the Ice Age. And it had been
left there as glacial debris for at least 10,000
years. History unfolded around it. It had been
part of the culture - especially, I think, the
child culture of that area - since earliest times.
Perhaps the earliest Paleo-Indian peoples had
felt its power. Perhaps their children, like me,

had climbed on it all the way back in the time when mammoths still roamed.

The adults in my neighborhood never knew that this was Elephant Rock — unless, of course, some child kindly told them its proper name and all about it.

Years later, when my children were growing up, I went back to my old neighborhood for an early morning walk and discovered that my boulder had been bulldozed away. That doorway into the imagination - into the dreaming of that specific place on the earth and to all that had happened there, into the life of natural things and into my own life as a child - was closed. I felt real loss and sadness and I realized that natural places, dreaming places all around the earth, are threatened daily. As we destroy them, we destroy the gateways to our own deepest potential for thinking, dreaming, and imagining. I realized that the only way I could pass this particular doorway on, pass on the experience of faith in the power of the dreaming, imagining mind which the boulder had given me, would be through a story. As a child, I had often wished that I could see a live mammoth. So, in the story, the Elephant Rock of my childhood became the mammoth of Will's. That's where the story of *The Boy Who Loved Mammoths* truly began.

In stories, wishes *can* come true. This is, in part, what makes them so important. Things that might not, could not happen in ordinary reality *do* happen in stories. Stories allow us to explore, experience, and make real archetypes of wish and dream — universal patterns of challenge and fulfillment. In our culture, we tend to discount this great power. The discovery of the hairs at the end of *The Boy Who Loved Mammoths* and of the flower at the end of *Will's Mammoth* are situations in which we all can remember the power of our own dreaming and imagining. "In dreams begin responsibilities," said the poet W.B. Yeats. So, too, all things we create in life begin with what we dream. The imagination, a realm of endlesss possibility, is the real foundation of our lives and accomplishments.

I'd like to mention something interesting that happened when I finished writing *The Boy Who Loved Mammoths*. You already know how Will is saved by a mammoth who stands over him, keeping him safe through the storm. Well, one night, while I was waiting in the car for my wife and watching the snow whirl down, I heard a story on National Public Radio's evening broadcast. They were talking about a little boy who had wandered out of his house - in Wisconsin, I think, or Minnesota; anyway, someplace rural and cold - during a bad storm. The boy's nine-month-old puppy was also missing — a big, shaggy puppy. Search parties had been sent out. They had been sure that when they found the boy, he'd be frozen to death. But when they found him, he was all right. The puppy had remained standing over him the whole night, keeping him warm. I watched the snow falling past the windshield, brightly lit against the street lights. And I thought, "So, it's true. I just wrote that story, and I didn't know if it could really happen. But it can. It did."

Not long after, I also discovered that Innuit peoples have tales about mammoths. They say that, long ago, a great shaman drove all the mammoths underground. That's why their bones and frozen carcasses are sometimes found close to the surface of the earth, as if they were coming back up to the surface. The legend also says that one night in every year, mammoths can return to live on the earth. So. you can see that *Will's Mammoth* and *The Boy Who Loved Mammoths* actually have a history going back much further than my own personal wishes and dreams.

Sharing this story in any version is a way of sharing my faith in the importance of our essential human powers to wish and to dream — a faith every child has. It's a way of saying that the imagination and its formal structures, stories, offer us a great gift: the restoration of our own Vision.

I've come to realize that I, like Will, am essentially a dreamer. I've been talking for years about *Will's Mammoth*, a dream of mine, and how it developed from the wishes and memories of my childhood in many keynote addresses and workshops accross the country. I have also touched on it a bit in my book, *A Storyteller's Story.* It's a relief to now have the original version out as a book, so that both adults and children can see what changes have actually occurred. And it's been interesting too, in communicating all of this, to realize just how deeply the dreams of our childhoods can inform our lives — our real, creative lives — as adults.

Good luck in your own dreaming, in your own writing and storytelling.

Rafe Martin
Rochester, NY - Fall 1995